BOY DOES TRASH FLY!

A Recycling Story

James R Thomas

Copyright © 2013 by James R. Thomas

ISBN-10: 149295828X

ISBN-13: 978-1492958284

LCCN: 2013921960

All rights reserved. No part of this book may be used or reproduced in any manner whatsoever without written permission, except in the case of brief quotations embodied in critical articles and reviews.

If you purchased this book without a cover, you should be aware that this book is stolen property. Neither the author nor publisher has received any payment for this book.

First Edition

It was a bright sunny day. Two brothers, Jeff and Tom, were walking home from the school bus stop when they came upon a piece of trash on the side of the road. Tom was the first to see the old soda can. Looking to have a little fun, he kicked the can, launching it high into the air. He then turned to his brother adding, "Boy does trash fly!"

When it was Jeff's turn to kick the old soda can, he extended his foot back behind him, ready to kick the old can with all his strength. However, he stopped just short of launching the soda can down the road. He instead picked it up and held on to it.

"Put that piece of trash back on the ground, so I can kick it again," said Tom.

But Jeff refused his brother's wishes and put the old soda can into his backpack, next to his school books.

Tom declared, "Jeff, you're no fun," shaking his head in disapproval of his brother's actions.

The two brothers continued with their walk home. Within a short distance, they once again came upon a piece of trash on the side of the road. Tom was the first to see the old worn-out piece of paper. It had black ink written on both sides, so he wadded it up and tossed it to Jeff saying, "Boy does trash fly!"

Jeff caught the old piece of paper with one hand, flattening it back into a smooth piece of paper again and put it into his backpack, next to the old soda can, and next to his school books.

Tom again declared, "Jeff, you're no fun," shaking his head in disapproval of his brother's actions.

The two brothers once again continued walking home. Within a short distance, they again came upon a piece of trash on the side of the road. Tom was the first to see the old glass bottle. He picked it up, extending his arm with the old bottle in his hand, as far as he could over his shoulder, ready to throw it far down the road. However, at the moment of release, his brother stopped him by grabbing the old bottle before it could be tossed away.

Jeff put the old bottle into his backpack, next the old worn-out piece of paper, next to the old soda can, that was next to his school books.

Tom again declared, "Jeff, you're no fun," shaking his head in disapproval of his brother's actions.

The two brothers once again continued their walk home. Within a short distance, they again came upon an object on the side of the road. Tom was the first to see the old newspaper and picked it up. He rolled it into a tube before tossing it down the road, end over end. He then turned to his brother, adding with a smile on his face, "Boy does trash fly!"

Jeff walked over to the old newspaper, picked it up, and placed it into his backpack, next to the old bottle, next to the old worn-out piece of paper, next to the old soda can, which was next to his school books. Tom once again declared, "Jeff, you're no fun," shaking his head in disapproval of his brother's actions.

Now down the road, the two brothers could see their dad at the end of the driveway to their house. Tom and Jeff waved, happy to see their dad. As they got closer, they could see a large blue container next to a normal trashcan. "Dad's taking out the trash," said Tom.

"That's not all trash," said Jeff.

However, Tom was too busy to take notice of Jeff's comment.

The dad seeing his two sons waved back, happy to see them home from school. "Hey boys, why don't you go into the garage and help me take out the rest of the trash."

Tom, following his dad's instructions, walked toward the garage to get the trash. However, he stopped after a few steps when he didn't see Jeff following him. Tom turned toward Jeff and said, "Dad asked both of us to take out the trash."

Jeff just looked at his brother, smiling as he opened his backpack. One by one, he pulled out the items next to his school books. He took out the old worn-out newspaper. He took out the old glass bottle. He took out the old-worn out piece of paper. He took out the old soda can, and handed them all to his father.

His father smiled and said, "Good job Jeff, you're keeping the earth clean by recycling old things instead of throwing them away." His father then placed the items in the blue recycle bin, so they could be recycled by the city.

As Jeff walked down the driveway toward his brother, Tom turned to him and said, "Jeff, do you think if we look through the trash, we might be able to find more things to recycle?"

"Sure!" replied Jeff.

And that's what they did, finding more things to recycle for their father. The father in turn placed them into the blue recycle bin, so the city could reuse them.

Their father was happy to see both his sons working together. After the two brothers finished their chores, they both went on another walk around the neighborhood, looking for old trash like paper, cans, and glass to recycle. They now were aware that they were important in helping keep the world clean by recycling old used up things, helping to reuse, reduce, and recycle everyday items around them.

THE END

ABOUT THE AUTHOR

James R Thomas published his first children's story in 2004. His writing style has been inspired by his military service and has developed into several series of children's books, to include science fiction, fantasy, conservation, and the deployment genres. Through his writing he addresses a variety of life issues for young readers, helping to cultivate strong minds. He is a graduate of the United States Naval Academy with a Bachelor of Science in Aerospace Engineering and he holds an advanced degree in Business Administration. James is married with a son and a daughter.

For more books by James R Thomas

Space Academy Series

Joe Devlin: And New Star Fighter, Book 1

Joe Devlin: And The Lost Star Fighter, Book 2

Coming Soon! Don't miss the next Joe Devlin book

Joe Devlin: In The Moon's Shadow, Book 3

Deployment Series

My Dad Is Going Away But He Will Be Back One Day

My Mom Is Going Away But She Will Be Back One Day

What Will I Play While You Are Away?

Coming soon! Don't miss the next book in the series,

We're Moving Today! A moving story.

Conservation Series

Boy Does Trash Fly!

Boy Does Water Run!

Coming Soon! Don't miss the next book in the series,

Boy Does Electricity Glow!

Visit James R Thomas paperbacks on the World Wide Web at https://sites.google.com/site/childrenpicturebooks/

Made in the USA
Charleston, SC
05 September 2014